I CAN READ ABOUT

HOMONYMS

The mystery of the hidden treasure

Written by Robyn Supraner
Illustrated by Joel Snyder

Troll Associates

Gene and Jean are twins.
They're always looking for
something to do.
What's going to happen
today?

Their teacher calls Gene and Jean the *Homonym Twins*. Their names sound alike, but their meanings are different.

"I'm not like Jean," says Gene.

Gene is a boy. He has light brown hair, blue eyes, and seven lucky marbles. When he speaks, he speaks very softly.

Jean is a girl. She has light red hair. Her eyes are brown, and she has seven freckles on her nose. When she speaks, she usually shouts.

They both take care of
their puppy, Edgar Allan.
Edgar Allan loves a
mystery. And so do Jean
and Gene.
And today, they're going
to *have* a mystery.

Their mother and father planned
a special surprise for them.
They planned a treasure hunt
with six clues to follow
and a treasure at the end
of the hunt. That would
keep everybody busy
all afternoon!

"Here's Clue Number One," said mother.
Mother handed them a little white card. The word FLOWER was printed on the card.

"Flower is just a part of the clue," she explained. "The rest of the clue is a word that sounds exactly like flower, but means something else."

"I know," shouted Jean. "It's flour!"

"It's a mystery," said Gene very softly. "And homonyms are the clues."

"You're right," said mother. "Now follow the clues."

"But where should we look?"
asked Jean.

"Which clues should
we follow?" asked Gene.
"Flour or flower?"

"Is it flour or flower?"

"Follow the clues," said mother,
refusing to say another word.
"I wonder where I should look,"
said Jean.

"I'm going to look in the flower garden," said Gene. "I bet the clue is there."

"Well, you look in the flower garden, and I'll look in the kitchen," called Jean. "You look in the flowers, and I'll look in the flour."

"One bug, two snails,
three lilies, four stones,
and no clues," mumbled Gene.

"Hey, I found it."
Jean came running across the
grass. She was holding a new card.
"I found it. It was under a box of
baking flour."

All this time Edgar Allan was helping, too. He was running back and forth.

Edgar Allan barked and
wagged his tail. He looked at
the little card and sniffed at it.
The letter U was printed on the card.
"What do you think that means?" asked Jean.

"Maybe
it
means
you,"
said
her
brother.

"Me?" laughed Jean.
"Well, if it is me,
I'll look myself over
and find the clue.
I'll look in my pockets
and under my shoe.
Oops . . . no card . . . just a hole.
It's not me," she said.
"It must be you."

Gene turned his pockets
inside out. He looked in the bag
with his lucky marbles.

"No luck," he said.
"It's not me."

Suddenly, Jean jumped up.
"I know. A ewe is a sheep, a
female sheep. The clue is a ewe,"
she shouted.

"Don't be silly," said Gene. "There are
no ewes in this town. There's just you and me . . .
and we're not solving this mystery."

The twins thought
and thought. Then
Gene jumped up, pulling
Jean after him.
"Come on," he said.

"It must be under the yew . . . the yew tree."
They ran to the small evergreen tree, and
hidden among its branches was a note.
The note said:

Please note this note.
The word is HORSE.

"We don't have a horse," shouted Jean.
"It could be a fake horse," said
Gene very softly.
"We don't have a fake horse, either,"
Jean shouted again.
"Stop shouting," said Gene. "Shouting
will make you hoarse. Then you won't
be able to speak at all."

Oh.
my ears

"HOARSE," shouted Jean at the
top of her lungs. "That's the answer.
The homonym for HORSE is HOARSE."

"I'm here . . . Don't shout.
I can hear you quite well.
    Now, where in the world
shall we look for a hoarse?"
said Gene.

"You can't put a saddle on this kind of hoarse," Jean mumbled. "Where shall we look for a hoarse?"

Edgar Allan was sniffing a bee
while she was thinking.

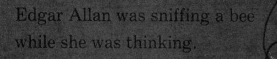

"I HAVE A GREAT IDEA!
Sometimes, when I'm hoarse, mother
gives me honey. Let's go find
the honey," she called.

They ran to the kitchen. And sure enough, right under the honey jar was Clue Number Four. The word on the card was TRUNK.

"An elephant's trunk? The trunk of a tree? An oversized suitcase? What kind of trunk can it be?" wondered Gene.

"Let's find out!
Let's hurry and look."

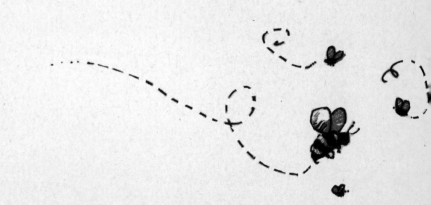

Jean rushed over to the trunk
of the apple tree, and touched the bark.
Edgar Allan just chased around, and barked at a bee.
But it was Gene who found the clue!

"It was in the steamer trunk," he called,
waving a small card. Clue Number Five was WHICH.
"What's a *which*?" asked Gene.

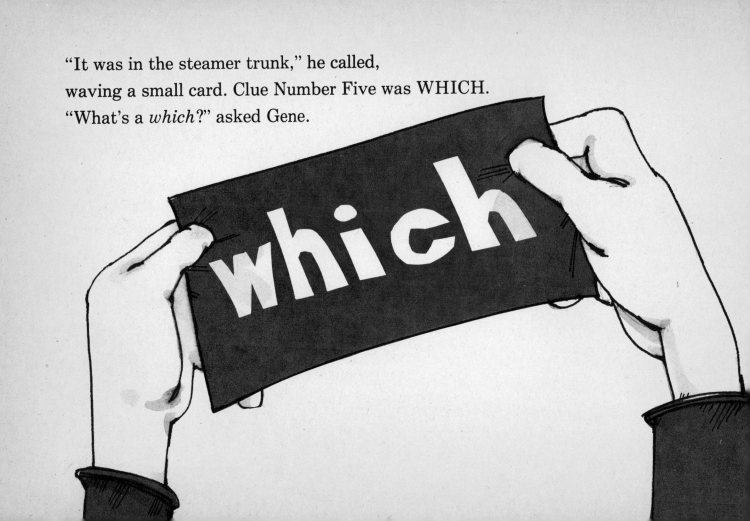

"Oh that must be a
wicked old witch,
like a Halloween witch,"
answered Jean.

"Heh . . .
. . heh . . . heh . . .
Which witch do you
mean? A mean,
old witch? Heh . . .
heh . . . heh."

"Cool it, you're
making the dog bark!
Stop cackling . . .
and think of
something *witchy*."

"Something witchy?
A broom is something witchy," said Gene.
And before you could say ghosts and goblins,
they found Clue Number Six in the broom closet.

Sure enough, inside the broom closet was a card. The final clue was HAIR. The twins were puzzled. They could not think of a homonym for hair.

"Hair?
Maybe it's just plain hair," said her brother,
"like in hairbrush, or hair ribbon, or shampoo."
     But no matter where they looked,
they could not find the clue that
would lead them to the
mysterious treasure.

Sniff. Sniff.
Edgar Allan started
scratching and sniffing
at an old straw basket.
"Edgar Allan, this is no time for playing."
But Edgar Allan continued to bark
and sniff and scratch.
"He's trying to tell us something," shouted Jean.
"Quick, open the basket and let's see what's inside!"

"A rabbit," they cried.
"It's a rabbit."

"Hair and hare," smiled mother. "A hare
is like a rabbit, only larger."

"Edgar Allan found her with his nose," said Gene.
"The nose knows," laughed father.

And that's just what they did.

The end of
the tale.